DEC
. 1998.

To Jakob —

Have fun learning the
alphabet! Best wishes —
Debbie Groesser

ALPHABET SOUP

· A Feast of Letters ·

ALPHABET SOUP
· A Feast of Letters ·

Written and Illustrated
By
SCOTT GUSTAFSON

THE GREENWICH WORKSHOP PRESS
Shelton, Connecticut

*Very special thanks to Patricia Olson for much hard work
and good counsel concerning the design and
overall appearance of this book*

Published by The Greenwich Workshop, Inc., One Greenwich Place
P.O. Box 875, Shelton, Connecticut 06484-0875
Distributed by Artisan, a division of Workman Publishing
708 Broadway, New York, NY 10003-9555

•

Library of Congress Cataloging-in-Publication Data:
Gustafson, Scott. Alphabet soup: a feast of
letters/written and illustrated by Scott Gustafson.
Summary: A host of animals from A to Z come to Otter's
housewarming party, bringing a wide variety of food
for his alphabetical soup. ISBN 0-86713-025-3
1. Animals--Fiction. [1. Food--Fiction. 2. Alphabet.] I. Title.
PZ7.G982127A1 1994 [E]--dc20 CIP:94-30729

•

•

Manufactured in the United States of America
First printing September 1994
10 9 8 7 6 5 4 3

THE GREENWICH WORKSHOP PRESS

To my parents, Dorothy and Maynard

Otter had just moved into his new house. It was empty except for some dust and a big old soup pot.

"I should have a house-warming party," he thought, "but what will I serve?"

Then Otter had an idea...

...Soon he was sitting on the floor, writing invitations to 26 of his closest friends!

Dear Friends,
Please come to my house for a "Pot Luck" party. I have a pot and if I'm lucky you will all bring ingredients for soup! If you don't have food that's soup-worthy then just bring food that you like! Come as you are!
Your Friend,
Otter

And this is who came...

ARMADILLO AND ASPARAGUS

A Armadillo was an award-winning archer who aimed asparagus arrows into the pot.

BEAR AND BREAD

...all these were bundled
into big baskets and brought
to the banquet by Bear.

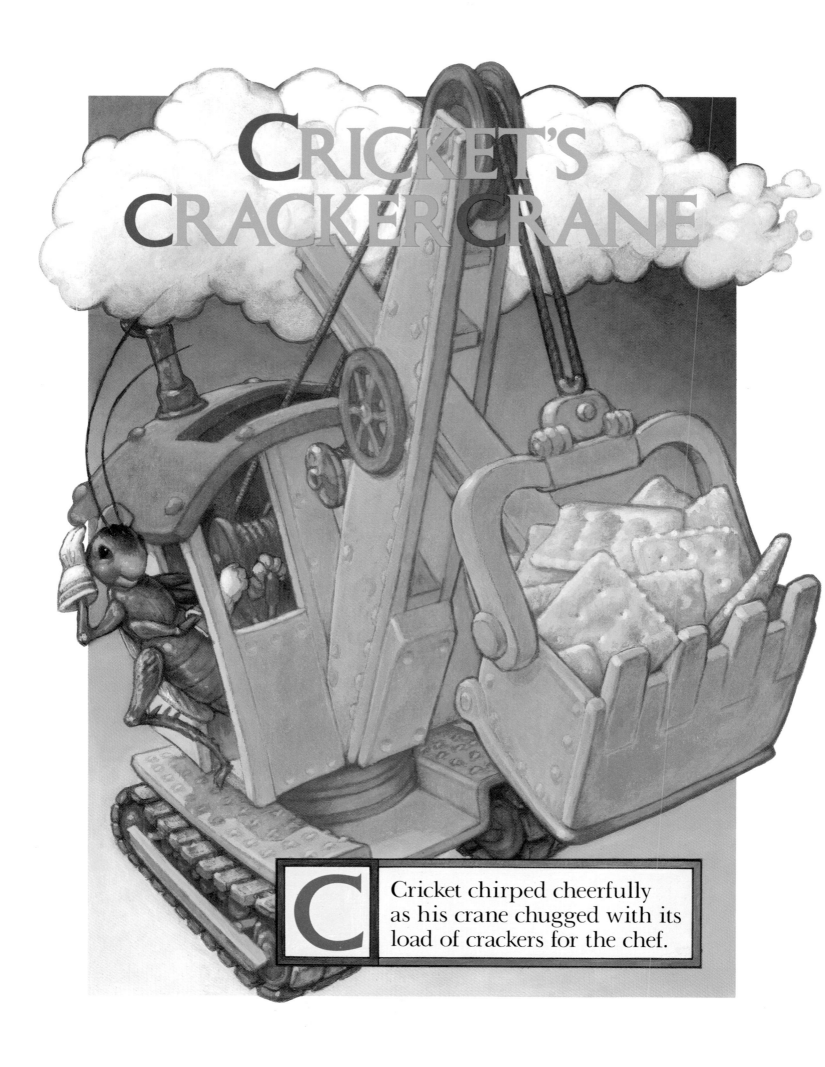

CRICKET'S CRACKER CRANE

C Cricket chirped cheerfully as his crane chugged with its load of crackers for the chef.

DRAGON AND DESSERTS

D Dragon didn't do dinner, so he delivered dozens of delicious desserts instead.

ELEPHANT AND EGGPLANTS

E Elephant enjoyed eggplants, which he carried in the folds of his elegant ears.

FROG FIXED FLAP~JACKS

F Frog had a flair for flapjacks, which he flipped and flopped in the frying pan.

GIBBON'S GARLIC GARDEN

G

Gibbon's gift was garlic, which he gathered from his garden in a golden goblet.

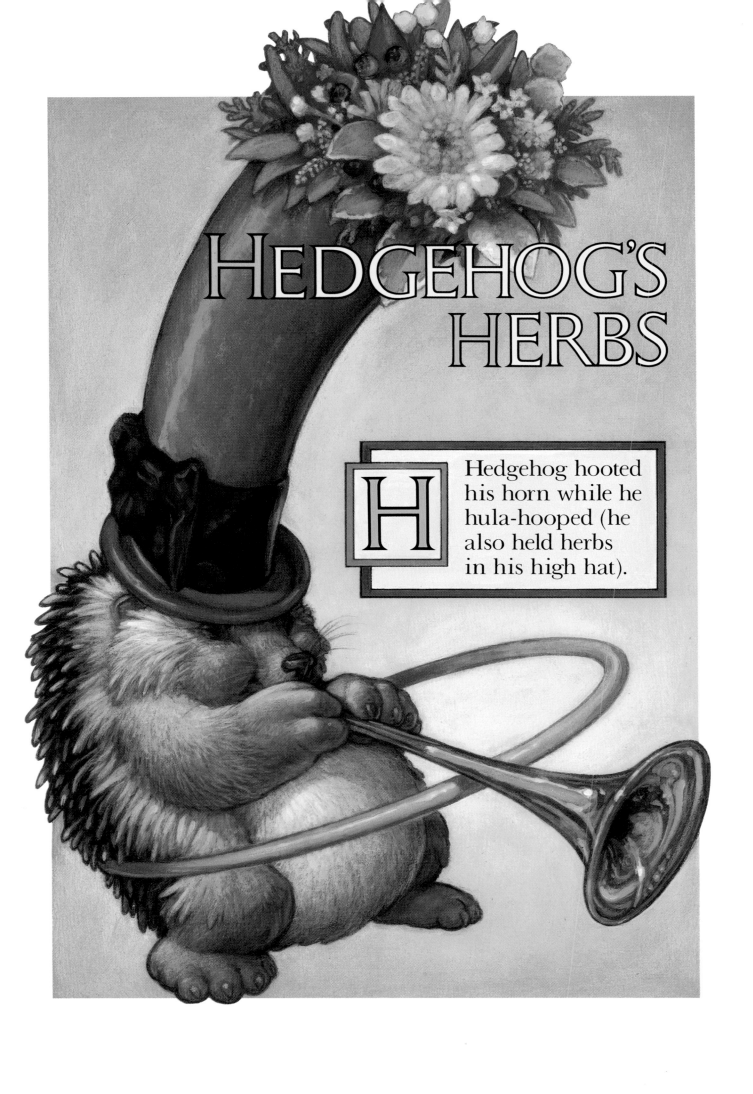

HEDGEHOG'S HERBS

H Hedgehog hooted his horn while he hula-hooped (he also held herbs in his high hat).

INSPECTOR IBEX

I Ibex insisted on inspecting all the ingredients before they went into the soup.

JAGUAR, JAMS AND JELLIES

J

Jars just
jam-packed
with jams
and jellies
were
jauntily
juggled
by a jolly
Jaguar!

K

Koala was kind of kooky—in a kerchief she kept kumquats, ketchup, and krill!

KOALA
KUMQUATS
KETCHUP and KRILL

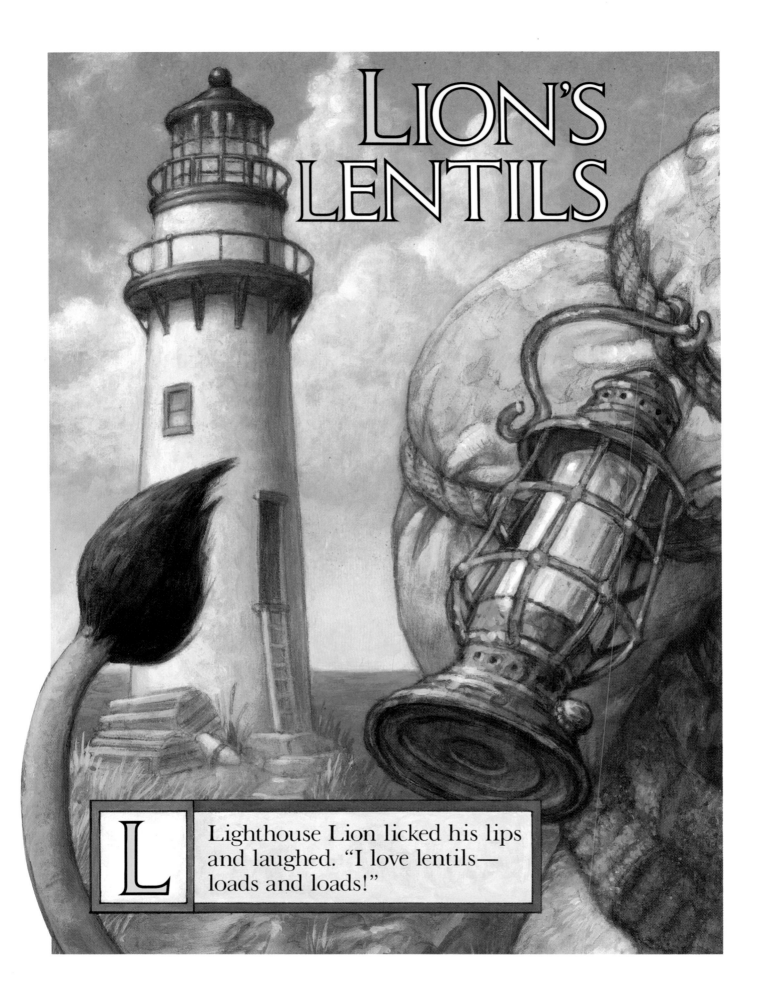

LION'S LENTILS

L Lighthouse Lion licked his lips and laughed. "I love lentils— loads and loads!"

MOLE'S MUSHROOM MINE

M Mole mines marvelous mushrooms. "Mmm, Mmm!" says he. "Me thinks a meal's a mess without 'em!"

NEWT'S NOODLE NET

N Newt was a nearby neighbor, who brought a net full of ninety-nine noodles!

OWL, ONIONS AND OKRA

O Owl offered oodles of onions and okra, and hooted out opera as well!

PIG'S POTATOES PARSNIPS AND PEAS

P Pig was a princely porker who proudly paraded his platter of potatoes, parsnips, and peas.

QUAIL AND QUINCES

Q A quart of quality quinces was carried by Quinella, Queen of the Quails.

REPTILE'S RUTABAGAS

R "Rutabagas roasted ranch-style" was the recipe of a rough-ridin' rip-roarin' Reptile.

S Squirrel stuffed his ship full of scallions, spinach, seasonings, and so on. Then he set sail in a salad bowl!

SQUIRREL'S SALAD

TIGER'S THINGS

T Tiger had a truckload of things—
a table, a toaster, teacups,
toothpicks, and a teapot.

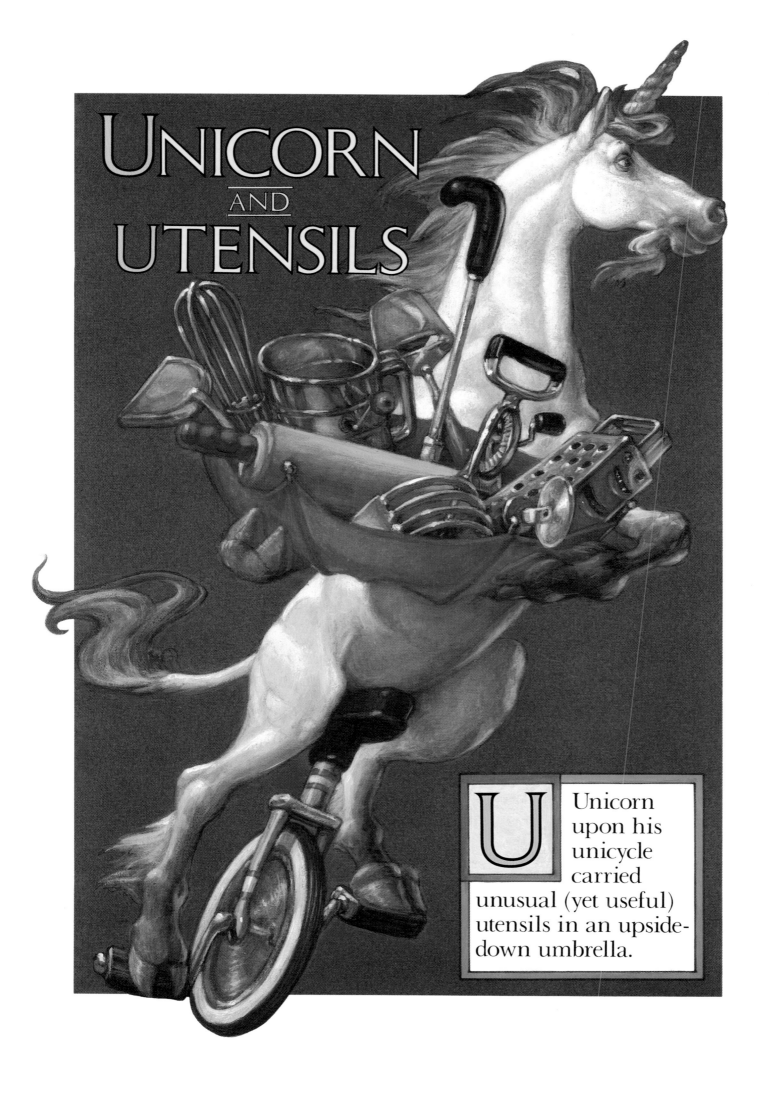

UNICORN AND UTENSILS

U Unicorn upon his unicycle carried unusual (yet useful) utensils in an upside-down umbrella.

VEGETABLES VIA VOLE

V "Vegetables have vital vitamins!" said Vole, "and I've got a vast variety available in my violin case!"

WEASEL'S WIENERS

W Wonderful wieners walked the wings of Weasel's Wizard Wagon, as he entered with the *WHOOSH* of a whirlwind!

OX AND XYLOPIA EXTRACT

Exported for Xanadu by one extraordinary Ox, the excellent extracts of the xylopia fruit made the mixture exciting and exotic!

As the pot full of ingredients simmered on the stove, Otter and his guests laughed and played party games.

Finally, it was time for someone to taste the soup!

They all held their breath while Otter sampled a spoonful.

How would it taste?

Was it going to be OK?

"It's delicious!" said Otter, "Everyone eat!" So they did. The animals had lots of fun eating the soup that they had all helped to make. But no one had more fun than Otter, because his old friends made his new house feel like home.